EDGES

Who is She?

Book 7

Bjorn Esterday Was Not Born Yesterday

Wynter Sommers

GJ dePillis

Published by Pure Force Enterprises, Inc.
California, USA
Since 2002

ISBN-13: 978-1-7184-0008-5
ISBN-10: 1-7184-0008-X

DEDICATION

To all of us whose hearts reach out to change the world around, whose minds calculate the next strategic move, whose souls crave adventure and value the freedoms of democracy. To the spirit harnessing the power of fiction to alter our reality, making the world a better place for everyone.

Bjorn Esterday Was Not Born Yesterday Series

Firebrand (9 Stories +Conversation Station Book)
Edges (9 Stories +Conversation Station Book)
Gone (18 Stories + 2 Conversation Station Books)

Bjorn EDGES Series
EDGES Book 1-Swift Encounter
EDGES Book 2-Rousing Attack
EDGES Book 3-One Foot Under
EDGES Book 4-Earthshake
EDGES Book 5-Broken String
EDGES Book 6-Key Witness
EDGES Book 7-Who is She?
EDGES Book 8-Vanish
EDGES Book 9-Chase or Die

Bjorn Series Alternate Reading Plan

1st   Edges Book 1
2nd Edges Book 2
3rd   Gone Book 1
4th   Firebrand Book 1
5th   Edges Book 3
6th   Firebrand Book 2
7th   Gone Book 2
8th   Gone Book 3
9th   Firebrand Book 3
10th Gone Book 4
11th Firebrand Book 4
12th Gone Book 5
13th Gone Book 6
14th Edges Book 4
15th Firebrand Book 5
16th Gone Book 7
17th Firebrand Book 6
18th Gone Book 8
19th Firebrand Book 7
20th Gone Book 9
21st Firebrand Book 8
22nd Gone Book 10
23rd Gone Book 11
24th Gone Book 12
25th Gone Book 13
26th Firebrand Book 9 (End)
27th Gone Book 14
28th Gone Book 15
29th Gone Book 16
30th Gone Book 17
31st Gone Book 18 (End)
32nd Edges Book 5
33rd Edges Book 6
34th Edges Book 7
35th Edges Book 8
36th Edges Book 9 (End)

CONTENTS

ACKNOWLEDGMENTS

To all those gentle souls who have graciously given tokens of love, hope, and kind considerations to others.

0 Preface

Pip Courtly, Skipper's son, is brought into the Soldier Police Headquarters as a "person of interest"

In the year 2032, we finally see where Elder James brings the Sisters and Widows, suggesting they settle in this new town.

After much hard work, the Widows and Sisters collaborate with the Earth Farmer Brothers, and create a "rest haven village", complete with an Inn to welcome weary travelers.

One year after building up the village in 2033, we see that it has taken months of toil and labor, but the Widows'

Cloister Sisters, along with the Monastery Brothers have worked together to make a productive settlement.

Queenie has become fully integrated into this society, adopting her new identity. She seems to be very comfortable with her new life and new name.

1 CHAPTER Year 2035: We Meet, Again (Continuous Ch 65)

The SP stopped on the side of the road. His head-lamps spot-lighted Jack. He closed the door behind him with a swish, then click. He walked quietly to where Jack crouched.

Jack, wounded and exhausted, stared up into the blinding lights.

The SP halted when he saw Jack's face.

"You're coming with me," he said as he helped Jack to his feet.

"Officer... What's the problem, now..." Jack mumbled.

1

Jack was eased into the vehicle's back seat. The door clicked shut, trapping him inside. Jack wondered vaguely why this officer didn't cuff him. He blinked as his eyes still saw white spots from the vehicle's blinding light beams.

Then, the officer slipped into the driver's seat and closed the door behind him. He turned around to look, through the partition, at Jack in the back seat.

Jack recognized him. It was that scowling guard from the men's prison!

It was Guard Gene.

"I just came from a village," Gene started, "where they said somebody tackled the AnCors and released children about to be sold at auction."

Gene turned around, took the wheel, and the vehicle started forward down the road.

"Yes..." Jack was cautious not knowing which way this conversation was going.

"I was assigned to investigate," the officer continued. "Those villagers had something all gift wrapped for me. It was one of the AnCors. He was scalded pretty badly. The villagers described a man when I questioned them. They said some wild man tackled the slave truck and rescued the children, single-handed. This stranger told the villagers he had to keep moving, but thanked them for their 'congenial hospitality'..." The SP glanced up at the rear view reflector, to look at Jack, and grinned, 'Congenial hospitality?' "

Jack said nothing

Gene continued, "Congenial hospitality... That reminds me of a prisoner who claimed to be a dead man when he checked in."

Jack remained silent. His heart beat faster.

Gene went on, "That newly captured AnCor told me Percy Snatcher, the one heading this recent AnCor slave round-up, was the one who shot me years ago during a train hi-jacking."

Guard Gene paused, waiting. Jack

3

maintained his silence. Guard Gene asked, "Didn't you also claim to be a passenger on that train? I wondered if the man described at the village might be you."

Jack still said nothing.

Gene made a right turn, onto a narrow road through the forest, and sped up.

"The fact remains," Guard Gene observed, "that you are still an escapee."

"Are you going to send me back?" Jack asked quietly.

Guard Gene stopped the vehicle suddenly. He sat for a long moment, thinking and staring straight ahead into the black night.

Then, he got out and opened up Jack's door from the outside, pulling Jack to his feet. Jack tensed, not knowing what to expect.

He faced Guard Gene and asked, "Is this where I am supposed to attempt an escape and you shoot me in the back?"

Guard Gene motioned for Jack to be silent.

"Listen," he whispered to Jack, "You saved my life during the Earthshake prison riot. And you just rescued a truck load of kids from being sold into slavery."

Gene continued, "So, I am going to drop you off. The villagers told me that they advised you to come here. It's just a few steps down that road, but it would have taken you another day by foot. With that leg, you wouldn't have made it."

Gene helped a limping Jack by wrapping Jack's weak arm over Gene's shoulder. They walked slowly down the pathway, flanked by shrubbery and trees. After a few steps, they came to a village clearing. Gene looked up and down the dark street.

Nobody was around.

Jack winced, dragging his wounded foot as they awkwardly stumbled toward the sign, "Earth Farmer Rest Haven Inn for Weary Travelers".

Gene eased Jack down onto the porch. Then, Gene reached into his own pocket and pulled out a small device.

"This has enough credits on it to pay for several nights here, and then get you to wherever you want to go. Good luck, friend." He clipped the device to the inside of Jack's shirt pocket.

"Thank you, Officer Gene," Jack feebly replied, slipping into unconsciousness.

Guard Gene tapped lightly on the Inn door. As soon as he heard rustling inside, he turned and strode away before they could see him.

He got into his vehicle and sped off.

Elder James, holding a lit candle, came outside to investigate the noise he heard. As he walked out onto the porch, he almost tripped over Jack's body. Slowly, he kneeled down to lower the light of his candle and see if the man on the porch was alive or not.

The man was breathing.

Elder James shook him. Jack did not

respond. Elder James was soon joined by another sleepy brother holding a candle.

The brother asked, "Is everything all right, Elder?"

Elder James replied, "This man surely qualifies as a weary traveler, Brother. Help me carry him inside."

The two men set down their candles and then lifted Jack Courtly. As they transferred Jack to a simple cot and brought candles into the room, Jack regained consciousness briefly.

Jack said, "Elder James?"

Elder James was taken aback at being recognized, but Jack's eyes closed. He was unconscious, again.

2 CHAPTER Year 2035: The Next Morning At Rest Haven Inn (Continuous Ch 66)

The next morning, Elder James greeted Jack with folded clean fresh work clothes for him to change into.

"These are for you, brother. The wash basin and towels are there. Breakfast on the side table there for you. When you are ready, join me outside on the porch," Elder James concluded as he closed the door to give Jack some privacy.

Jack washed up and changed clothes. It felt so good to finally put something clean on his body. Hungrier than he realized, he devoured every scrap of food they set out for him. After a few moments, he joined Elder James on the porch.

The center of town was already humming with activity around the Inn.

"And how are you feeling, my son?" Elder James asked.

"Much better, Elder James," Jack replied as he crossed the porch and took a seat next to Elder James.

"I must say, I do not recognize you. How is it you knew my name before I introduced myself to you?" Elder James asked.

Jack smiled and looked down. Ah, yes, he'd have to explain.

"You see, you would come by the men's prison to feed us. The last time I saw you, I helped you out with..."

Elder James, now remembering, finished his sentence, "...with my supplies. Yes. That was the evening of the Earthshake back in '32."

9

Jack nodded, "Three years ago."

"That evening changed the future of many people," Elder James mused.

"Yes..." Jack looked out onto the bustling center of this new town. It seemed to be quite lively. He turned to Elder James and asked, "That day you told me you had run short of food and had to stop by the cloister to enlist the aid of the sisters there."

"Yes?"

"You had a woman with you. I am looking for that woman. Can you tell me where she is?" Jack asked.

Elder James stood abruptly, stepped back and glared at him. "Sir! We are not here to supply your carnal needs. No! The sisters must be respected."

"You misunderstand," Jack explained. "The woman I am looking for could be my wife. Her name is Queenie Courtly."

"We don't have any sisters or widows by that name to my recollection," Elder James firmly stated.

"Please. Listen. We were on a train together," Jack continued. "An Earth Farmer woman sewed several quilts my wife designed." Jack reached into his pocket, pulled out a tattered scrap of fabric, and explained, "It was this pattern she sewed. Have you seen this pattern before?"

Elder James stood there, staring at the tattered cloth.

Jack continued, "I have prayed I could find my wife again, Elder James. Please, will you help me? Does this cloth look familiar to you?"

"There was a train accident five years ago," Elder James started, "but I am not certain I have seen that cloth pattern before."

Jack inhaled deeply. He remained silent for a moment, looking down at the ground, then said, "It was worth a try. So, would you happen to have a razor, Elder James? I would so very much like to shave off this heavy beard. And bandages?"

11

The Elder nodded at Jack and beckoned him to come inside, "We can provide both those things for you."

3 CHAPTER Year 2035: Who Is She (Continuous Ch 67)

Elder James was showing a now clean-shaven Jack Courtly around the small village. Jack hobbled along with his still painful wounds freshly bandaged.

When they approached the center of the village, by the well, Jack was impressed to see a crude plumbing system of pipes freshly laid in shallow trenches waiting to be covered up to allow horses and wheeled vehicles to ride over the network of water piping. The structure of the pipes seemed to radiate out from the well to supply water to the

13

larger buildings in the area. These people certainly were creating a livable village.

A park had been built up around the well. In the park were a number of vegetable beds. Some of the women were planting small trees. Others were trying to get the vegetable beds prepared for planting.

One woman was digging up the soil with a pick ax to break the hard dry earth. The next woman came by to smash down dirt clods. Another followed sprinkling what looked like fertilizer.

Then, came one who hand-plowed rows into the earth. Another followed by laying tubing and snaking it up and down each row, stapling it into the soil with large four inch hooped spikes to anchor the tubes to the ground. Yet another made sure one end of the tube was firmly connected to one of the pipes from the well. With a crude lever on each row, water could be turned on or off as needed.

Finally, another woman came by

holding a jar of seeds, kneeling in the earth, pushing in one seed, then another, then reaching into her pocket and pulling out a small sign identifying those seeds. Then, she set the jar aside and went back to the end of the row and picked up another jar of seeds, doing the same thing on a different row.

This woman intrigued Jack from a distance.

"Elder James, who is that woman setting out seeds?"

"That is the cloister's gardener. Widow Medicina," Elder James replied.

"Would you introduce us?" Jack asked.

Elder James asked a question to answer Jack's question, "Are you offering your assistance in setting up the garden?"

As Jack nodded, a frantic brother rushed up to Elder James and said, "Elder James, Come quickly! Come now!"

"What is it?" Elder James demanded.

"North Town is diverting the river, which feeds our well. You must speak with their mayor immediately or we won't have water as of this evening!"

Apologetic, Elder James rushed off, saying, "I'll be back as soon as I can." Elder James and the brother hurried away, leaving Jack standing there by himself.

Jack wondered what to do. It had been so long since he saw the woman he thought was Queenie, but this time Jack was clean shaven so he hoped his appearance wouldn't frighten her, as it had at the men's prison. If this was the same woman.

The woman stood up, then took a small cloth from her pocket to mop her brow. She replaced the quilt square into her pocket.

Upon seeing her with the quilt square, Jack's heart raced and he found it difficult to swallow. He took a couple of steps toward the woman, then hesitated. He reached into his own pocket and extracted the tattered quilt square he'd been carrying with him for so long.

He took a few more steps toward her, then stopped again several feet away.

She must have sensed somebody watching her. She turned around, facing him, and stood there, squinting.

"Hello?" she asked. The brim of her bonnet shaded her eyes. "Can I help you? Are you lost?"

For a moment, Jack couldn't speak. Then his voice cracked, "Queenie?"

She gasped.

He said nothing more.

They both stood looking at each other. It had been years. Harsh, tragic, trouble-filled years.

With a confused expression, Queenie took a step toward him. He took a step toward her. For a moment, Jack felt as if nobody else were around. He forgot they were in the public garden.

Slowly, he extended his hand with the

quilt square. Queenie brought her hand up to her mouth, surprised to see what he was holding.

Jack asked, "Did you drop this? Back at the cloister?"

Jack wondered, did she recognize him? He held his shaking hand out, offering the quilt square. Slowly, Queenie reached and plucked it from his hand, careful not to touch him. She glanced at the square, then into Jack's eyes, then back at the fabric, again.

With her other hand, she took out the square she had just used to mop her brow. Queenie held both squares up together to form a unique larger pattern, just as Ruth Lantz had stitched together on the train so long ago.

Jack spoke softly, "Queenie, you remember me. Jack. Your husband. Don't you? You remember this pattern you designed for Ace's quilt, right?"

She stood, frozen, looking down at the squares, not at Jack. Was she remembering?

Silently, her eyes met his and welled up with tears as her lips tried to form the word, "Jack?"

"Yes," he replied relieved, opening up his arms, welcoming her hug if she chose to give it. Queenie did not respond. Jack dropped his arms. They both stood in silence for a moment.

"At the prison? Was that you?" Queenie's voice trembled.

"Yes," a single tear traveled down Jack's cheek.

Queenie took one step toward him. "But, we had to leave the cloister. The AnCors took over our home. Elder James never... He never went back to the prison after the Earthshake. How did you find me?"

Queenie took another step closer to Jack.

"God allowed our paths to cross, Queenie. I can't explain it."

Then, she rushed into his arms, clinging to him tightly. With a sigh of relief, he wrapped his arms around her. He had his Queenie back. God gave him his Queenie back.

"The train," Queenie started, "...you disappeared from the train. I looked for you. Where did you go?"

"It's a long story." He kissed her on the top of her head, cradling her in his arms, "Where is Ace?"

Queenie looked up at him.

"Ace?"

Jack frowned at her, perplexed. "Isn't Ace with you? In this village?"

Queenie took a step back, breaking free from his embrace, and whispered, "Jack, darling. Help me figure out how to stick the edges of these two pieces together." She focused on the two quilt squares.

Jack took her hands, folding each one around the fabric swatch she held in her clenched fists and looked into her eyes.

"Ace?" was all he asked.

Out tumbled a torrent of mixed emotions from Queenie's mouth. "I saw Ace's jacket. So much blood. Where did Ace go? Has the porter seen Ace?"

Jack crushed his wife to him, holding her close. He rested his chin on top of her head, fighting back his own tears as Queenie trembled in his arms. He had assumed all along that Ace was with Queenie. Now, he realized that Ace might not even be alive.

He was torn with grief and frustration, realizing the anguish they both had endured these past years, thankful he was reunited with his wife.

That would be enough for now...

4 CHAPTER Year 2036: Dinner at Sarah's Condo- Who Is Knocking? (Continuous Ch 68)

Realizing Bjorn said he would zip right back, Sarah figured she might as well get ready for dinner.

Assuming Bjorn would bring food, she thought maybe she could make some chocolate ice cream, if she had all the ingredients.

In her tiny kitchen, she found 12 ounces of bittersweet chocolate and dropped it into a saucepan with some sugar. She had just enough milk, a pint, to pour over the chocolate and simmer it on her little stove. Then, she removed the pan from the heat and added three egg yolks, carefully saving the whites for breakfast tomorrow. She figured if she didn't have cream with her tea that night, she could use it for the ice cream. After letting the mixture cool for a few minutes, she added chilled cream and stirred. Finally, she poured the warm velvety mixture into a bowl, then popped it into the freezer. They'd have chocolate ice cream in a few hours. The very idea made her feel exuberant.

Then, grabbing two plates and two glasses, she set them out on the coffee table in the living room. She decided to make herself a cup of black tea while waiting for Bjorn, so went back into the kitchen to put on a kettle of water to boil.

The visual news chattered away in the background. Now having completed the story about Skipper and Pip Courtly, it was on to other less interesting events of the day. She returned again to the kitchen to pick up salt, pepper, napkins and utensils.

There was a knock at the door.

Sarah quickly placed the utensils down in the center of one plate and went to open the door, expecting to see Bjorn, but was greeted instead by another visitor.

The tea kettle whistled.

5 CHAPTER- Year 2036: Where Is the File? (Continuous Ch 69)

"Oh, hello!" Sarah started, "you are just in time to join me for a cup of tea, if you like. Please come in."

Sarah smiled as she held the door open for her visitor, Alexandra Lantz.

"You just missed Bjorn. He should be back shortly with dinner. He said he enjoyed the office tour you gave. It was brief, but...well, none of us want to think about what happened that day..." Sarah smiled as she guided the intern, Alexandra, to the sofa.

Alexandra smiled politely.

"Have you come to finish up what you shared with me at the hospital?" Sarah

25

asked as she prepared two cups of black tea, offering one to Alexandra. Sarah sat next to Alexandra on the sofa.

"Yes. I didn't mean to scare you on the evening you were admitted, Miss Paradise." Alexandra spoke softly as she accepted the piping hot cup.

"I forgot you told me you volunteered at the hospital after our last one-on-one session at the office," Sarah remarked.

"So, you understand that I had to keep the lights out. I couldn't risk being seen talking to you," Alexandra explained.

Sarah blew on her tea to cool before sipping it. She nodded her head that she understood, now.

Alexandra continued, "You see. I had prayed God would lead me to a person I could trust."

"Trust? With what?" Sarah asked, curious.

"After what you had gone through at the castle. I mean, since you never told Pip that I was the one who gave you those papers..." Alexandra struggled for words, "Oh, I am so sorry you lost your job because of me, Miss Paradise. I know you almost lost your life. I hope you don't think me too silly, but I don't believe it was an accident. And I know you really are the only one left who can help me. Help us. Will you?"

Sarah was caught off guard, "Help you? With what? Alexandra, I can't help with any of those Courtly Corporation issues."

"But you can!" Alexandra pleaded.

"I just lost my summer income," Sarah tried to explain. "If I make trouble, they could legally make me lose my teaching position, as well. I've even heard that if you make trouble for a large corporation like Courtly, you might just disappear. I'm so sorry. I just can't risk being a statistic. I know all the Earth Farmers are upset about the toxic waste being dumped on their farmlands, but I honestly don't see how I could possibly help." Sarah shook her head.

Alexandra glanced at the visual news Sarah had on display, with the volume low.

"What do you think about Pip Courtly being arrested for his father's murder?" Alexandra asked.

"I don't think Pip has been arrested. The news said Pip is helping the SPs with their inquiries. Besides, it's not my affair. I mean I suppose if the SPs have reason to bring him or anybody in for questioning, they must know something that I don't..." Sarah replied.

"Miss Paradise. I'm not sure you can expect the Soldier Police to be completely impartial. They are paid by the corporation, remember? I'm not a fan of Pip's but he could have been framed for murder," Alexandra said.

Sarah paused mid-sip with her tea cup up to her lips. She placed the cup down on the table in front of her. Alexandra took a sip of hers as she waited for Sarah to reply.

"Purely as an academic exercise," Sarah suggested, "tell me why do you think a self-centered wealthy playboy would be framed for killing his father? Maybe he needed more money. Maybe he was tired of waiting for his inheritance."

"I don't admire Pip," Alexandra started, "but I can't see Pip killing anybody... especially not Skipper Courtly, his own dad."

"And why do you draw that conclusion, Alexandra?" Sarah asked the young woman.

Alexandra reached into her quilt bag to bring out a cloth covered object. She handed it over, indicating Sarah should unwrap it.

"What is this?" Sarah asked. Sarah carefully took off the cloth concealing the device. Inside was an old game unit. The word "Prototype" was clumsily written in marking pen on the body. Sarah shrugged in reaction.

Alexandra started to explain, "I think that Pip Courtly is innocent because time was running out."

"Running out?" Sarah asked.

"You see, Miss Paradise, Pip and Skipper Courtly never actually collected the inheritance from the former CEO, Jack Courtly. Instead, they were advised to use the promise of inheritance as collateral, convincing all the vendors to essentially work for free in the hopes of getting paid this year."

"Whoa, Alexandra. Everything they have purchased in the last six or seven years has been on borrowed money? They are in debt?"

"Precisely," Alexandra explained, "Pip inherits a huge gaping debt. Right now, Pip doesn't have a single credit." Alexandra placed the cup of tea on the table in front of her.

"Pardon me for asking," Sara started, "but when you began to tell me this in the hospital, I was in no state to listen. But, for a simple intern, you are impressively astute. The vocabulary you are using right now is a good deal more sophisticated than when we spoke regularly in the office," Sarah observed.

Alexandra just sat there with her

hands folded in her lap, eyes cast downward, not answering.

Sarah looked again at the unit in her hands, "So, why bring me this thing?"

"I found it..." Alexandra's voice trailed off as she squirmed uncomfortably.

Sarah saw that Alexandra seemed uneasy about revealing more information.

"Is that it? You found an old game that your community wouldn't permit you to play with, anyway?"

"I am not an Earth Farmer," Alexandra started. "I may dress or act like one simply because I have been living with them for some time, now."

"Well," Sarah prompted, "I might be ignorant about esoteric customs, but if you have lived with them... I mean if they did accept you into their closed community... and don't take this the wrong way, but shouldn't you, as a young woman in that society, be quilting, not apprenticing full-time at a large corporation?"

"True," Alexandra Lantz replied simply. Alexandra withdrew from her bag, a small patch of quilting. The pattern was unique. The quilt was small enough to be a placemat.

"I did this... See? I can quilt. It's just that I also want to see justice done."

"I'm still," Sarah struggled to form her words, "missing some dots to connect. This isn't making sense to me. Why are you, a country girl who doesn't even attend the Courtly school system, an intern at Courtly Dynamics Corporation?" Sarah took a long look at a silent Alexandra. "You do know how to intelligently blend in with whatever environment you find yourself."

Alexandra paused, thoughtful.

Sarah sipped her tea, waiting.

"I took the position," Alexandra said, "to investigate why Skipper Courtly violated a long term agreement with the Earth Farmers, which had been set up by Jack Courtly... why Courtly Corp is funding this Mayfounder Foundation research for bio-weapons, cloning, and other mysterious projects... why Skipper Courtly is running up huge bills and can't pay off the vendors from corporation profits. Where is the money going? Why does he have to use Jack Courtly's will as collateral to keep borrowing?"

"I've not heard of this Mayfounder whatever. Besides, why would you care how some corporation spends their money?" Sarah asked.

"My adopted Earth Farmer family's livelihood depends on me to get them some answers about stopping the toxic dumping. Please understand, Miss Paradise, I owe them for taking me in."

Sarah looked at the device in her hands as she asked, "Right. I see. Destroying the Earth Farmer crops will eventually trickle down to the city citizens and impact our food supply, as well... So, you are adopted, then?"

"Not officially," Alexandra replied.

Sarah understood. During these war-torn years, widows and orphans were in abundance. For survival, people moved in with each other. Not everyone had the luxury of registering the necessary paperwork. Sarah nodded.

Alexandra continued, "My parents died and an Earth Farmer family took me, an orphan, in as their own."

"I can understand your appreciation for a family assuming the burden of another mouth to feed in these chaotic times, Alexandra, but even I know that to live with them, you need to live in accordance with their customs. How do I say this..." Sarah paused, then decided for the direct approach, "Earth Farmers don't play electronic games of any kind. Why didn't the community make you give this up after you found it?"

"True. To live with them, I adopted their customs, but they let me keep this as a reminder of my parents."

Alexandra reached over to turn the device on, pressing a button, which was hidden. Sarah looked at the device as it beeped to life. On the screen appeared several legal, looking documents.

Then, Sarah looked more closely at the document that was now actually displayed on screen.

"Hey!" Sarah burst out surprised, "This file is the one that got me fired. You told me you found this in the paper files, but this is the soft copy. You printed this out, didn't you? How did you get this?"

At that moment, there was a knock on the door. Sarah got up informing Alexandra, "Bjorn said he'd be right back. He's probably bringing enough food for us all to share. I know he'd be very interested in your story, Alexandra. Would you stay and join us for dinner?"

"Thank you, yes." Alexandra smiled and took a sip of tea.

Sarah went around the corner to the door and opened it, but it was not Bjorn.

"Sarah Paradise?" The official looking SP stated, visor down, expressionless.

"Yes," Sarah stated factually, her heart was beginning to thump.

"We suspect riots will sweep this way and you have been asked to evacuate."

"Evacuate?" Sarah paused, cocking her head to listen, hearing nothing, "Officer, I don't hear any crowds rioting. I've had the visual news on for quite some time and there has been no mention of it."

Then the SP pushed his way past Sarah, into her living room.

"Excuse me, Officer, but I don't recall giving you permission to enter my home."

"Orders. Where is the file?"

"What?" Sarah stammered, "What file?"

The officer saw the two partially set dinner place settings. He barked at her, "Where is your guest."

Sarah, seeing the officer zero in on the two plates, looked around, but didn't see Alexandra. The prototype device was gone.

"I set the table, expecting my friend to come by. He will be here soon," Sarah explained.

The SP checked her tiny kitchen, then headed to Sarah's bedroom. Sarah held her breath. The officer burst in, but the room was empty. He pulled blankets and pillows aside, looked under the bed, slid open closet doors. There was nothing to find.

Sarah wondered how Alexandra had vanished so quickly.

"Officer? What are you looking for? Why are you here? If you are conducting an official search, I need to see your authorization."

The officer pawed through Sarah's desk, ignoring her. Opened the second bedroom and tore it apart. Sarah used that as her home office. Desk drawers were yanked open. Papers were flying. Cushions were overturned. It was a sloppy flustered job.

Then, he suddenly stopped as if receiving a communication. He paused, facing Sarah, as he listened to his com device.

"She is alone, sir. No copies found. The one he originally took from her must be the only copy."

Without apology, this militant whirlwind stalked out, leaving Sarah in the middle of a very messy abode.

Infuriated, Sarah slammed the door shut behind him.

She immediately marched to her com device, put it in her ear, and contacted Soldier Police headquarters.

"Yes. I would like to file a complaint. You sent an officer down here to evacuate my condo because of a riot. Yet, there doesn't seem to be any riot outside. Your SP barged in and searched my place! He refused to show me authorization and tore my place apart!"

The SP receptionist on the other end of the phone placed Sarah on a brief hold, then replied, "We don't have any notifications of riots, nor orders for any citizens to evacuate and, Teacher Paradise, our records show we have not dispatched an officer to your residence.

Are you sure he was an SP officer?"

"Uh...I'm not..."

"Was anyone hurt?"

"Well, no, but..."

"Do you wish to demand an investigation of this issue? Since this incident does not involve any Soldier Police activity, the fees for an investigative service will commence from the inception of your verbal report..."

"Fees...?"

"Yes, Teacher Paradise. At what time precisely did the ..."

"Uh... wait...You mean you will dock my credits for filing this report?"

"Yes. This is not an SP personnel issue. You are filing a complaint of an intruder, correct? There is a fee for that."

Sarah recalled her shrinking credit balance. "I don't need... Can I cancel this whole report thing... I'm sure it was just a mistake on his part."

"Yes, madam. Are you canceling?"

Sarah tried to swallow. "Are there any fees?"

"Not now that you have canceled. Do you want to cancel? Please confirm, Teacher Paradise."

"Please... cancel..." Sarah said reluctantly.

"Of course, Teacher Paradise. Disconnecting Comms." The SP receptionist ended transmission.

6 CHAPTER Year 2036: Only Witness (Continuous Ch 70)

Alexandra, surprisingly athletic, dropped to the ground with her quilting bag over her shoulder. She was quick on her feet. She had scrambled out of Sarah's bedroom window and down the shadowy fire escape, as soon as she heard it was not Bjorn at the door.

This SP's voice boomed authoritatively.

She could hear every word he said. She pressed herself into a dark corner behind some shrubbery and watched until the SP emerged from the building's entrance.

He did. But, he did not enter a Soldier Police vehicle. One was parked nearby. Instead, he walked around the corner. Alexandra decided to follow from a distance, ducking into the shadowy crevices formed by the angular architecture of surrounding buildings.

She held her breath as she saw the man pause in a deserted area. He leaned against the brightly colored shreds of an old billboard near a pile of debris and removed his helmet visor, tossing it casually onto the heap. It was a fake. It didn't have the complex electronics inside the lining of the helmet that she had seen with other Soldier Police.

Alexandra recalled that the SP uniforms morph and camouflage, mimicking the colors the uniform would touch. But, when this SP leaned against the wall his jacket remained the same. The colors didn't change. He ripped it off, tossing it on the pile as he looked to make sure nobody was around. Then, he jogged away down the street.

Alexandra remained hidden, continuing

to watch.

A couple of blocks down, Alexandra observed this same man get into a large expensive idling vehicle. After about two minutes, he emerged again, holding a package. She couldn't see the person inside the vehicle and she couldn't see all the identifying markings on this vehicle.

It was too far away.

She understood what this meant. This man had just been paid. He was no Solider Police. And she knew exactly what he was looking for.

She wasn't about to let him get it.

7 CHAPTER Year 2036: Analyze This (Continuous Ch 71)

The night was getting colder, and Alexandra didn't know what to do. Should she go back to Sarah's place? Yet, she had caused that poor woman so much trouble. She began to feel guilty. What were her options?

She loitered in the neighborhood until she saw Bjorn park in the parking lot of Sarah's building and get out of his vehicle.

She called quietly to him from the shadows, "Mr. Esterday."

He turned around as she beckoned to him. "Remember me? I was your tour guide at the office?" Alexandra said.

He moved cautiously toward her voice.

"Yes. I remember you," Bjorn replied recognizing Alexandra's face as she stepped out from the shadows into the dim glow of the parking lot lights, "What can I do for you?"

"Sir, Mr. Esterday, Sir..."

"Yes?" Bjorn asked.

"I know you have only just arrived, but I must tell you, Miss Paradise has had an unpleasant visit."

"I'd better go see if she's OK, then." Bjorn became concerned, walking more briskly toward Sarah's building entrance.

Alexandra trotted behind him. "She's all right, now, but I need to show you something." She opened up her bag to reveal the fake helmet and jacket that the false Soldier Police wore when searching Sarah's condo.

"Wait a minute. What is that? An SP uniform? Where did you get that?"

"I have a request, Mr. Esterday, bringing this evidence with us up to Miss Paradise, now may upset her. She's already been through enough. Besides, the aura prints on this SP uniform may dissipate if you don't get it scanned in time."

"You'd better explain," Bjorn walked back to his vehicle and opened the door for Alexandra. She got into the passenger side.

"I'm listening," he said bluntly.

"These are from the man who just visited Miss Paradise, claiming to be a Soldier Police. He wasn't. I believe that somebody wanted to make sure that Miss Paradise didn't have an extra copy of the papers that got her fired... and quite possibly drowned at the castle."

"And you know this because..."

"Because the man who wore these never saw me, but I heard everything he said. I'm confident he believes there are no other copies and just wanted to get paid," Alexandra clarified.

"He believes? You mean there are other copies?" Bjorn asked.

"If you get fingerprints, DNA, or aura print off these items, and identify the wearer, I'm sure you'll be able to connect him to his boss, the person responsible for setting all this up."

Alexandra handed the quilting bag containing the helmet and the fake Soldier Police jacket to Bjorn.

"You'll have to get them processed quickly. I'm sure whoever the boss is will be making plans to leave this area very soon," Alexandra warned.

"Let's go now. Keep talking." Bjorn started up his vehicle, as he made a com call, "I need to ask you a favor... Yup... another one. Great. See you soon. Bye."

His vehicle hummed along the road. Alexandra kept talking.

"I have a device that looks like an old fashioned toy, but it contains copies of Courtly documents dating back seven years. Some even earlier than that. Legal and financial documents. It's proof."

They moved through traffic, Bjorn carefully obeying every signal. He didn't want to be stopped.

"Proof of what?" Bjorn asked.

"That Skipper Courtly never should have been running things for the last seven years," Alexandra announced.

"What?"

"He was a puppet guided by corruption and greed."

"That sounds a bit melodramatic. Not a lot of people were a fan of Skipper Courtly, but I'm gonna need to see proof of your accusations," Bjorn stated.

"I've got a document showing Jack Courtly's original signatures supporting the Earth Farmer communities, setting up factories to be run by the Earth Farmers, and providing workers from the city to man the electrical equipment that Earth Farmers wouldn't touch. Factories run with clean energy to avoid polluting the earth God has gifted us with. Certain agreements promised that toxic waste would be processed and recycled or dumped far away... Definitely not on the very land that grows food that you would be eating."

"But Jack Courtly died..." Bjorn protested as he drove, "...things change with new management."

"And the week he died, a second will, a forged will came out, giving Skipper Courtly full run of all the corporations owned by Jack. It was supposed to have been run by... other more responsible and competent people..."

"How do you know the second will was forged?" Bjorn inquired, his voice cool.

"Jack may have had a fight with his brother a few days before his train trip. He must have searched the databases for files, thinking he could examine them during his trip. On the device I just told you about, he had copies of documents postdated and already signed, but those signatures were really different from all the other Jack Courtly signatures that came before…" Alexandra clenched her fists, "Forged!"

"Well, with Jack Courtly dead, why are you so upset they put the brother, Skipper, in charge?" Bjorn asked.

"I'm not upset Skipper being in charge. I'm frustrated about blatant violations of contracts and financial trickery," Alexandra defended.

"Like what?"

"Okay. For example, one employee started out as a contracted worker making 50 credits an hour seven years ago. But the week Jack Courtly died on that train, there was a forged order to increase this particular employee's pay to 500 credits an hour!" Alexandra paused, "Then, when I was interning, I worked in payroll, and found he is now making 2500 credits an hour? In seven years, is it possible to go from 50 to 2500?"

Bjorn pulled up to their destination. He ran in, taking along the quilting bag containing the helmet and jacket. In a few minutes, he reappeared and returned the empty quilting bag to Alexandra, then resumed driving.

"Now, we should head back to Sarah. They'll call me if they find anything."

Bjorn and Alexandra headed back toward Sarah's place. On the road, as they moved along, Alexandra suddenly pointed out the window.

"There it is! That's the vehicle!"

"What vehicle?" Bjorn asked, senses heightened.

"The one that paid off the man pretending to be a Soldier Police." Alexandra almost yelled, "He's turning the corner!"

"Let's see where he is going..." Bjorn got out of his lane and gingerly wove around other vehicles until he was about three hundred yards behind the car.

"You know, Alexandra, you could have

just gone to the Soldier Police station with this."

"I did, Mr. Esterday," Alexandra explained. "I marched right into the Soldier Police station, but they wouldn't even look at what I had. They told me to take my concerns to the Elders of my village because Earth Farmers don't pay for Soldier Police protection. The corporation does. I didn't want to risk drawing any more attention to myself. I didn't know if whoever is behind all this has paid off some of the SPs, so I didn't want to endanger my own investigations by being a pest."

Bjorn suppressed a smile. This kid was either telling the absolute truth or she had a great imagination. He'd have to see this device she was referring to.

The car they were following made a sudden sharp turn.

And disappeared.

"Where did he go?" Bjorn asked himself. Then, glancing in his rear view reflection surface, he saw that same mechanical menace was now coming up behind him.

"You are harnessed in, right?" he snapped to Alexandra.

"Yes. Why?"

"Because I think the hunted just became the hunter..."

8 CHAPTER Year 2036: Who Is Driving (Continuous Ch 72)

"That driver must be paranoid. How does he know we're not just traffic?" Bjorn said more to himself than to Alexandra, "Does he think we are following him?"

"We are following him, aren't we?" Alexandra asked.

Then, the car tapped Bjorn's bumper from behind.

Bjorn sped up.

Keeping pace with Bjorn, the ominous vehicle pulled up beside him, remaining in his blind spot on the driver's side. Then, with a sharp, bump, it dented Bjorn's side panel.

"What?!" Bjorn exclaimed.

Alexandra braced herself, "There is another one!" she shouted.

Another car came up and flanked the passenger side, forcing Bjorn to speed ahead of both cars attempting to sandwich him in.

Bjorn jerked his car away, turning sharply to evade both pursuing vehicles. Alexandra squeezed her eyes shut.

"Do you have this proof device on you? Is that why they are after us? Are they tracking you?" Bjorn demanded.

"No!" Alexandra yelled over the screeching tires, "They can't possibly know where the device is."

"Are they tracking you?" Bjorn repeated.

"No. I don't have anything on me they

could track. They didn't find what they were looking for at Miss Paradise's place, so I'm guessing they think she gave it to you! Or maybe they just don't like you following them!" Alexandra shouted, straining her voice, her knuckles white as she gripped the restraint harness.

A warehouse loomed up before them. Bjorn aggressively drove straight for it. Outside was a wall of neatly piled bales of hay. Bjorn swiped the wall of animal feed and the wall of hay tumbled to the ground, blocking the path for one of his pursuers.

"Look back and see if you can find any identifying marks on those bad boys," Bjorn barked.

Alexandra turned her head around and looked at the other vehicle, obscured by fallen blocks of hay.

"It's not moving! Trying to start, but can't. Buried under straw," she shouted.

The second vehicle relentlessly hounded Bjorn, who sped up straining the mechanics beneath his hood. Then he suddenly slammed on his breaks and spun around 180 degrees, facing his attacking vehicle.

Alexandra's head bumped against her window, but the safety harness kept her locked in.

The other driver, not expecting Bjorn's move, skidded to avoid hitting him head on. Bjorn, now facing his opponent, could see through the windshield and make eye contact with that driver.

To his surprise, the driver's seat was empty. It seemed to be on auto pilot! Operating by remote control.

The wheels on the attacking vehicle shifted 90 degrees and, like a crab, moved sideways, then straightened out and abruptly zipped down a side alley, and sped off.

After catching his breath, Bjorn pulled back over to the wall of hay where the other vehicle had crashed.

Nothing. It was gone.

Hay was all over the place, but the

vehicle had just vanished. Bjorn stopped and got out. Alexandra didn't move. He searched the scene and found a piece of outer shell, picked it up, and slid back behind the wheel.

"What is that?" Alexandra asked as Bjorn put on his harness.

"I don't know. Could have been cracked off from one of those jerks," Bjorn sneered. "Could be trash that was already there. I just don't know what AYFO means. I've never heard of that brand."

"I'm no expert in vehicles, Mr. Esterday, I'm sorry I can't help you," Alexandra apologized.

"Maybe I can find out who builds a tactical vehicle that could be operated remotely. Something that can move like that must be expensive!" Bjorn determined.

"Now, maybe we should inform Miss Paradise about what is going on, Mr. Esterday?"

Bjorn glanced at Alexandra. "Right."

They headed back, driving with great caution, now. Bjorn's vehicle was clearly struggling to keep moving. It gasped each time Bjorn idled. Fragments of the body scraped against the road, creating sparks as they drove along. Drivers from other vehicles shot perplexed looks as they passed by.

Bjorn waved his hand to connect a call to a local restaurant, placed an order and said he'd be by in five minutes to pick it up.

"Should you file a traffic report?" Alexandra asked.

Bjorn shot back, "I need to find out who it was, first. They may have just reacted and don't know it was me they tangled with. If I file a report now, my identity will be shared with the other party, whoever they are, and they may try another attack. I'll wait until I know more."

"I see," Alexandra said quietly.

"I've ordered plenty of food. Would you like to join us for dinner or can I drive you back to your village?" Bjorn offered.

"No. I can't have the village be connected in anyway with what went on tonight. I already informed my family that I was visiting Miss Paradise. They don't expect me back for another day."

"Okay. Do you want to come inside while I pick up the food or wait here?" Bjorn asked.

"Mr. Esterday. I won't be here when you get back, but I know how to get in touch with you and Miss Paradise. I will see you later."

9 CHAPTER Year 2036: Is the Invitation Still Valid? (Continuous Ch 73)

Bjorn looked around Sarah's apartment, "They really made a mess here."

Bjorn dropped the bag of food onto Sarah's kitchen table, and began unpacking their dinner. Sarah, meanwhile, continued to straighten up the living room, salvaging the plates and utensils she had started to set out earlier.

"One guy did all this mess," Sarah fumed. "When I called the SP headquarters to complain, turns out he was a fake. He was after something, but I don't know what." Sarah shook her head. She could not stop trembling. She was becoming nauseated by a growing pounding headache. She was determined not to pass out.

"Where was Alexandra during all this?" Bjorn asked as he helped Sarah set food out on the table.

"She just vanished. I have no idea where she disappeared to," Sarah explained in a whisper.

Bjorn looked around.

He examined the kitchen, the bathroom, Sarah's spare bedroom office, and then her bedroom.

"A-ha!" Bjorn exclaimed.

"What?" Sarah asked.

"This must be how she slipped out, see?" Bjorn pointed to Sarah's window with the edge of the curtain partially caught inside.

"Oh, of course," Sarah added, trying to appear calm. "She must have trapped the corner of my curtain when she closed the window behind her. Why didn't I see that before?"

"Smart kid," Bjorn commented, "If she left the window opened, that fake SP would have looked out and maybe seen her on the fire escape. He never realized Alexandra was here. I can fill you in on the rest over a dinner." Bjorn gave Sarah a hug.

"I just feel there is much more to her story, Bjorn," Sarah said.

"I'm sure there is, but she knows how to get in touch…"

At that moment, there was a light tapping at the bedroom window.

Bjorn moved quickly to the window, pulled the curtains aside, and opened it.

There was Alexandra.

"Mr. Esterday invited me to dinner. Is the invitation still valid?" she asked.

"Yes, of course," Bjorn opened the window wide, pulling the curtain aside as Sarah helped Alexandra through. Sarah shut the window, locked it, and closed the curtain.

10 CHAPTER Year 2036: Where Did You Go? (Continuous Ch 74)

Bjorn asked Alexandra, "Where did you go?"

They sat around the table, eating as they spoke.

Alexandra replied, "I wanted to be cautious. I waited to make sure nobody followed you into Miss Paradise's apartment, and I took the back way just be make sure nobody saw me. That restaurant was only two blocks away."

Sarah asked, "And all this because of your device?"

"Here is what happened," Alexandra started. She took a taste of Bjorn's delicious restaurant food, savoring every bite. The spices blended into a hypnotic aroma. This is not the sort of meal she would have with the Earth Farmers. Now, she was very hungry after the evening's stressful encounters.

"Yes? Go on..." Bjorn coaxed.

"My mother," Alexandra continued, "searched for a fabrics artist in the Earth Farmer communities to redecorate a cottage my father had just purchased."

Alexandra held up the place-mat sized quilt she showed earlier.

"Did your mother design that pattern?" Sarah asked.

Alexandra nodded.

Finishing up her meal, Sarah, now

becoming filled with nervous energy, asked the two if they'd like some dessert. Still participating in the conversation, she moved to her kitchen to grab some ingredients.

"Dessert anyone?" Sarah excused herself explaining, "Cooking helps me calm down."

Bjorn frowned and called, "Sarah you should be here. Relax. Oh, OK. I forgot. You prefer to bake"

He nodded to Alexandra. "Please go on with your story."

In a mixing bowl, Sarah put one cup of butter, five tablespoons of sugar, two cups of light flour, two tablespoons of vanilla, two cups of pecans and a dash of water to make it stick together.

She put the dough onto a baking sheet, and popped the cookies into her oven at 325 degrees for eight minutes, until the undersides turned brown. Then when they were done, she rolled them in powdered sugar.

"Yes. We went on a holiday vacation and our train was attacked..." Alexandra stared down at her folded hands.

"Attacked!" Bjorn, repeated, surprised.

"Hi-jacked, actually, by somebody. My mother stayed on the train to help my father, who was assaulted by a waiter. I later found out my parents were killed. I escaped with an Earth Farmer family. On my way off the train, I grabbed my father's briefcase, which I had hidden in the train corridor earlier. That is how I got the device in the first place," Alexandra stated.

"You were running for your life and you grabbed a briefcase?" Bjorn asked.

"At the time," Alexandra explained, "It didn't seem real. There was a game on that thing, and I had stashed the briefcase away so I could get to the game later when my parents wouldn't see. It's hard to explain, but at the time, the train attack seemed like part of my game."

"Oh, I understand that," Sarah piped in, "Several kids in my classes who play virtual reality games have a hard time understanding that when you get killed off in real life, you don't just get up perfectly healed and come back to play another round."

"And where," Bjorn asked, "is this magic device?"

"I thought Miss Paradise would have found it by now," Alexandra said. She jumped up and hurried away into Sarah's bedroom, bringing back a winter boot. She turned the boot upside down and out slid the electronic unit.

"You hid that in my shoe?" Sarah asked.

"Yes, Miss Paradise. I didn't think he'd look there and I figured if they didn't find it on you, they would eliminate you as a trouble spot," Alexandra offered.

Bjorn asked, "When did the train hijacking become real to you?"

Alexandra thought a moment, "Only later... I realized the gravity of what happened."

Bjorn asked, "Tell me how you met the Earth Farmer family..."

Alexandra was silent for a moment, thinking.

"My mother ordered me to go with Mrs. Lantz because my father had been hurt. My mother said she would come for me later. Before we ran off the train, Mrs. Lantz told me to take off my jacket because it was too fancy. There was no way I wanted to do that! It was new. Even my cousin wanted to take it away from me. But, Mrs. Lantz won, and before we ran, that jacket was tossed aside so I could look more like an Earth Farmer."

"And that's when you started to adopt the customs of those people?" Bjorn asked.

"I guess. When I first arrived at the Earth Farmer's home, I thought everything was stupid and plain and boring." Alexandra shook her head, "I can't believe I actually thought that way about the people who had saved my life." She paused, then said, "It was only much later that we heard everybody on that train had died in the accident. And I realized then it wasn't a game. That those who died on that train would not be coming back with a new and different set of powers to navigate another virtual game."

"Why didn't you go back to the city and find an aunt or other family member to stay with?" Sarah asked.

"The news said 'accident', but the Lantz family warned me to lay low. Safety. They told me if somebody killed mom and dad, why wouldn't they kill me? The

Lantz family, who saved me, thought I would be safer if they kept me. And if I kept a low profile. They suggested I go by my real first name and... drop the Courtly..."

Bjorn held a hand up for Alexandra to stop as he asked, "You're a Courtly!?"

Politely, Alexandra replied, "Yes, Sir. The Lantz family begged me never to say my real name. I took the Lantz's last name and promised to live as they do... until my real mother could come get me, as she promised."

"When did your mother come to get you?" Sarah asked.

Alexandra's voice cracked, "She never came. She died on that train."

Then Bjorn's com device started to flash.

"Pardon me, ladies..." Bjorn muttered as he got up and went into the kitchen to take the call.

Sarah asked, "Alexandra, you've had such a fright tonight. All of us have. Would you like to stay the night in my guest room? I could make you baked clouds tomorrow morning, if you like. I would appreciate the company."

Alexandra started to say, "My family knows I came to see you, but it's a long way to travel home so I was planning on spending the night at an Inn."

Sarah protested, "An Inn? No. Please stay here and save your credits. I'll call the Inn and cancel and they can get word to your village that you'll be with me."

Alexandra considered, "As a single woman, it would be appropriate for me to stay in my own room in the home of another single woman, but wouldn't I be interrupting you and Mr. Esterday..." Alexandra looked at Sarah for a response.

"Oh goodness, no. Mr. Esterday is a gentleman and he has always acted honorably. He wouldn't spend the night here. He'd never want the neighbors to gossip," Sarah assured.

"In that case," Alexandra acquiesced, "I do thank you for the invitation and will accept. May I ask, what is a baked cloud?"

"Oh," Sarah started, "Well, it's something my grandmother used to make. One simply mixes half a cup of flour, half a cup of whole milk, three or four large eggs, unsalted butter...and you bake it in a large iron skillet. It's hard to find one of those these days. Bake at about 425 for just under a half hour or until it's puffy like a cloud. Then serve it dusted with powdered sugar, butter, lemon wedges or syrup."

Bjorn's results were in on the jacket and helmet he had just dropped off, his caller informed him. The fake SP now had a name, and Bjorn just needed to confirm who that man worked for.

He made another call.

Sarah, seeing Bjorn was still on his com, turned to Alexandra, "I've got to ask you something."

"Yes?" Alexandra replied.

"If you really are a Courtly, why did the articles covering the memorial service for Jack Courtly mention his wife, Queenie and their only child, Ace. No Alexandra..."

The unassuming country girl nodded her head, understanding.

"Miss Paradise, My nickname is Ace. It stands for my initials: Alexandra Carina Emmeline. A-C-E. Ace. If you need proof of my true identity, I was registered in the pedigree database when I was born."

Sarah got comfortable in her chair and asked, "Is that where all the corporation families are logged and traced?"

Alexandra replied, "Yes. I am confident

that if you compare my genetic print to Skipper or Pip, you would find we are closely related."

Bjorn, half listening to their conversation, called to Alexandra from the kitchen, "So did you get into all this today to prove you are a Courtly?"

Alexandra shook her head, "No. I did not come here to prove I am a Courtly, nor to try to fight Pip for any inheritance. I must struggle to accept that the crimes committed against my family have not and probably will never be punished. I came here, on behalf of my village, to ask for help, to allow us... the Earth Farmers... to grow food we all can eat."

Bjorn emerged from the kitchen, smiling, having completed his conversation and disconnected his com.

"I've made some progress," Bjorn announced, "and have to leave to check on something." Bjorn, paused and kissed Sarah on the head, then asked, "You gonna be all right here?"

Sarah nodded, forcing a smile, "I just hope this namby-pamby Lifestyles story doesn't kill you, Bjorn. I mean I'm a nervous wreck."

"I am as well, Miss Paradise," Alexandra added. "I am glad to stay here this evening and depart for home in the morning."

Bjorn headed for the door.

"Oh! Wait! Mr. Esterday," called Alexandra. "I think I've figured out who controls those vehicles that tracked us tonight." Alexandra jumped up, reached into her bag and pulled out a small square piece of cardboard, which she handed to Bjorn. It looked like a business card.

"Please take this, Mr. Esterday."

Bjorn accepted it, then the smile faded from his face. He looked at Alexandra, then at Sarah.

"Lock the door behind me, Ladies, and keep all the windows shut tight."

Then he was gone.

Sarah rushed to the door, locked it, and barricaded it with a chair, just in case. She leaned against the wall for a brief moment, then Sarah turned to Alexandra and asked brightly, "Want some chocolate ice cream and cookies?"

16 CHAPTER- What will happen next?

The AnCors, although now free themselves, are making money by kidnapping children from various areas and selling them at the slave market.

Dealing with these attacks, the Earth Famers are reminded of Proverbs 17: 15: 'Acquitting the guilty and condemning the innocent--both are detestable to the LORD.' (New Living translation)

We see that Jack, very weathered, now, risks his life, again, to save innocent children from a fate he himself almost endured –being sold into slavery. Earlier in the story, while on the train during the AnCor attack, Jack takes a bullet Percy Snatcher intended for Earth Farmer Noah Lantz. Will Jack's constant acts of selflessness eventually get him killed? When will he learn to just take care of himself... or do his acts of selflessness actually encourage others to watch out for him when he needs it. Which way would you behave? Will Jack be forced to confront the man, Percy Snatcher, who has been the cause of all this pain: the slavery market, the train attacks, etc... or will Percy keep getting away with his crimes?

The Earth Farmers share Galatians 5:22. 'But when the Holy Spirit controls our lives, He will produce this kind of fruit in us: love, joy, peace, patience, kindness,goodness,faithfulness, gentleness and self-control' (Living Bible translation).

Who is the mysterious visitor from Alexandra's village? Is Alexandra being truthful about what she reveals to Sarah, or is this another puzzle of lies for Sarah to uncover? What are the consequences to Bjorn? Should Sarah ignore this new information or act on it? If she does act on it, will she endanger her life? How should she decide what to do? What is the real issue: Toxic dumping? Who should be ruling from the Courtly throne? Worker rights? Fair treatment of Courtly citizens? What would you do?

.What surprising place will Sarah go to, to get her answers?

.What will Sarah, Bjorn and Alexandra do with the new information they learn? If they turn the information over to the wrong people, all three of them risk a quick and sudden death.

ঙ **To Be Continued...** ෬

17 Did You Know

Automobiles traditionally have been fueled by gasoline, but there are other engineered designs.

There are cars which run on compressed air, where the "exhaust" is cold and can be used for air conditioning. This motor has zero pollution.

In 2012, Nevada allowed the operation of autonomous cars. The first self-driving license was issued in May 2012 to a modified Toyota Prius. The software modification involves turning over the computerized and mechanical functions of the car to a virtual chauffeur which makes driving decisions.

A man named Sebastian Thrun, a director at the Stanford Artificial Intelligence Lab helped Google build the first virtual chauffeur to create a driverless car in response to a DARPA challenge back in 2011. To help with navigation, the modified cars have maps of the world along with other 3D maps to allow it to drive and guide itself.

English Clergyman, Thomas Bayes, developed a mapping navigation technique back in the 1700s.

His technique is known as the "Bayes Rule", which is to have world maps and detailed maps of the immediate area available together.

ORC International held a survey and found that 33% of the people surveyed said they would only buy an autonomous car if it had a self-parking system that would automatically park in a space for them. This may involve rotating the tires

45 degrees to 90 degrees to allow parking against a curb on the street.

88% said if they had to buy such a car, they would want to have a built in lane-departure warning system to inform them when they are drifting into another highway lane.

77% say they want a forward collision warning system that would apply the breaks faster than a human would, so that a crash could be avoided.

70% say they want special cruise control to maintain the distance from traffic ahead of them. What are your thoughts?

Some people want to feel the control of driving a car themselves. Others want to view driving as a way of getting from A to B so they would prefer to abdicate the responsibility of actually driving and allow the computerized chauffeur to guide their vehicle.

18% of the people interviewed in the ORC survey, said they would purchase a self driving autonomous vehicle. Out of that 18%:

Only 22% feel comfortable having their family driven in an auto-piloted car.

66% said they would not feel like a real driver in such a car, just going along for the ride. They want to be more engaged when driving.

They also say they are convinced that human error is the reason behind 90% of all crashes. They believe a computer won't be susceptible to wandering thoughts; it won't get distracted during a tedious commute; and it won't fall asleep at the wheel. Computers are ideal drivers, they say, and will make a safer road for everyone to drive on.

1) Computer reaction time is faster than human.
2) Computers don't get distracted or bored.
3) Computers don't fall asleep.

4) Computers won't run a red light.
5) Computers won't tailgate the car in front.
6) Computers won't do drugs.
7) Computers won't drink alcohol, then foolishly attempt to drive.

ABOUT Wynter Sommers

Wynter Sommers is the pseudonym for an American writing team, which harnesses multiple skills in technology, research, and education. Formally trained with a PhD in Education, Wynter Sommers blends academic classroom experience, with corporate sophistication, and a passion for developing more effective student insights.

Wynter Sommers has taught classrooms of enthusiastic children. She has a heart to inspire creativity and develop critical thinking skills, all to encourage students to make wise choices in life. She wants to impart the talent of honing one's skills in self-reliance and collaborative team work. Despite any environmental barriers outside of an individual's control, Wynter Sommers wishes to impart the message that genuine hope, love, and peace can help us overcome obstacles, and cement friendships. Wynter Sommers hopes you enjoy the other ***Bjorn Esterday Was not Born Yesterday*** stories in this series.